MARGARET WISE BROWN'S
THE SAILOR DOG

Pictures by
GARTH WILLIAMS

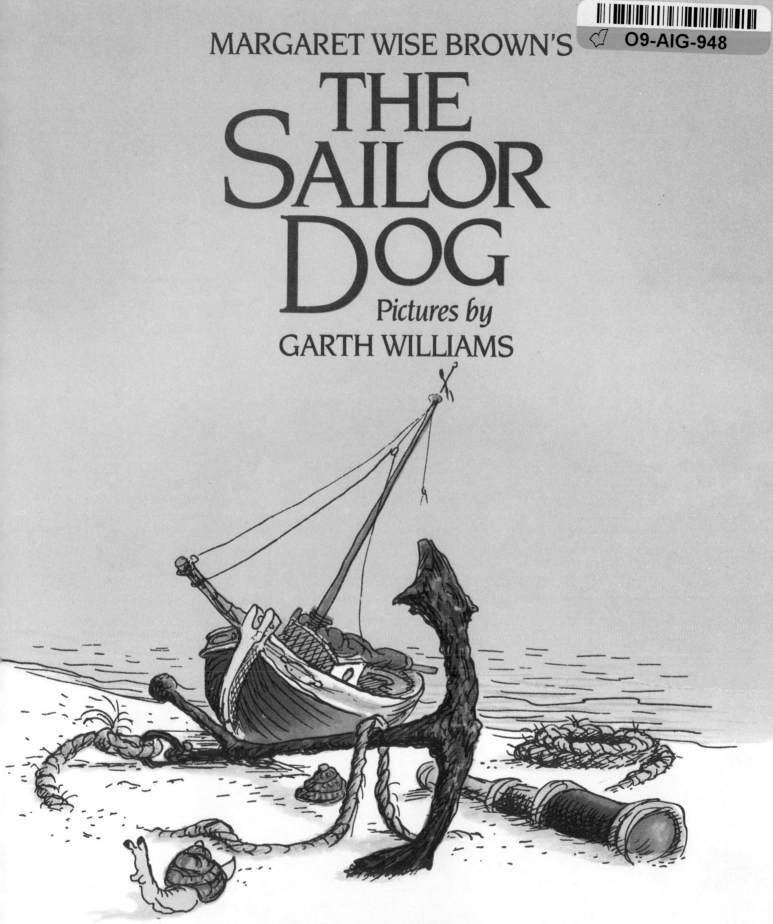

A GOLDEN BOOK • NEW YORK

Western Publishing Company, Inc., Racine, Wisconsin 53404

Born at sea in the teeth of a gale, the sailor was a dog. Scuppers was his name.

After that he lived on a farm. But Scuppers, born at sea, was a sailor. And when he grew up he wanted to go to sea.

So he went to look for something to go in.

He found a big airplane. "All aboard!" they called.
It was going up in the sky. But Scuppers did not want
to go up in the sky.

He found a little submarine. "All aboard!" they called.
It was going down under the sea. But Scuppers did not
want to go down under the sea.

He found a little car. "All aboard!" they called.
It was going over the land. But Scuppers did not want
to go over the land.

He found a subway train. "All aboard!" they called.
It was going under the ground. But Scuppers did not
want to go under the ground.

Scuppers was a sailor. He wanted to go to sea.

So Scuppers went over the hills and far away until he came to the ocean. And on the ocean was a ship. It was blowing all its whistles.

"All aboard!" they called.

"All ashore that are going ashore!"

"All aboard!"

So Scuppers went to sea.

The ship began to move slowly along. The wind blew it.

In his ship Scuppers had a little room. In his room he had a hook for his hat and a hook for his rope and a hook for his pants and a hook for his coat and a hook for his spyglass and a place for his shoes and a bunk for a bed to put himself in.

At night Scuppers threw the anchor into the sea
and went down to his little room.

He hung his hat on the hook for his hat, and his rope on the hook for his rope, and his pants on the hook for his pants, and his coat on the hook for his coat, and his spyglass on the hook for his spyglass, and he put his shoes under the bed, and got into his bed, which was a bunk, and went to sleep.

Next morning he was shipwrecked.

Too big a storm blew out of the sky. The anchor
dragged and the ship crashed onto the rocks. There was
a big hole in it.

Scuppers himself was washed overboard and hurled
by huge waves onto the shore.

It was foggy and rainy. There were no houses,
and Scuppers needed a house.

But on the beach was lots and lots of driftwood,
and an old rusty box stuck in the sand.

Maybe it was a treasure!

It was a treasure—to Scuppers.

It was an old-fashioned tool box with a hammer and nails and an ax and a saw. Everything he needed to build himself a house. So Scuppers started to build a house, all by himself, out of driftwood.

He built a door and a window and a roof and a porch and a floor and some walls, all out of driftwood.

And he found some red bricks and built a big red chimney. And then he lit a fire, and the smoke went up the chimney.

After building his house he was hungry.
So he went fishing.

He went fishing in a big river. The first fish
he caught never came up. The second fish he caught
got away. The third fish he caught was too little.
But the next fish he caught was—just right.

That night he cooked the fish he caught,
and the smoke went up the chimney.

Then the stars came out and he was sleepy.
So he made a bed of pine branches.

He jumped into his deep green bed and went
to sleep. And as he slept he dreamed—

If he could build a house
he could mend the hole in the ship.

So the next day at low tide he took his tool box
and waded out and hammered planks across the hole
in his ship.

At last the ship was fixed.

So he sailed away until he came to a seaport in
a foreign land.

By now his clothes were all worn and ripped and
blown to pieces. His shirt was torn, his hat and coat
were gone, and his shoes were all worn out. Only his
pants were still good.

So he went ashore to buy some clothes at the Army and Navy Store.

First he bought a coat. He found a red one too small. He found a blue one just right. It had brass buttons.

Then he bought a hat. He found a purple one too silly. He found a white one just right.

He needed new shoes. He found some yellow ones too small and some red ones too fancy. Then he found some white ones just right.

Here he is wearing his new hat and his new shoes and his new coat with the shiny brass buttons. (He has a can of polish and a cloth to keep them shiny.)

And he has a new rope and a bushel of fresh oranges.

Now Scuppers wants to go back to his ship. So he goes there.

And at night when the stars come out, he takes one last look through his spyglass. And goes down below to his little room.

He hangs his new hat on the hook for his hat, and he hangs his spyglass on the hook for his spyglass, and he hangs his new coat on the hook for his coat, and his pants on the hook for his pants, and his new rope on the hook for his rope, and his new shoes he puts under his bunk, and himself he puts in his bunk.

And here he is where he wants to be—
A sailor sailing the deep green Sea.

HIS SONG

I am Scuppers The Sailor Dog—
I'm Scuppers The Sailor Dog—
I can sail in a gale
Right over a whale
Under full sail
In a fog.

I am Scuppers The Sailor Dog—
I'm Scuppers The Sailor Dog—
With a shake and a snort
I can sail into port
Under full sail
In a fog.